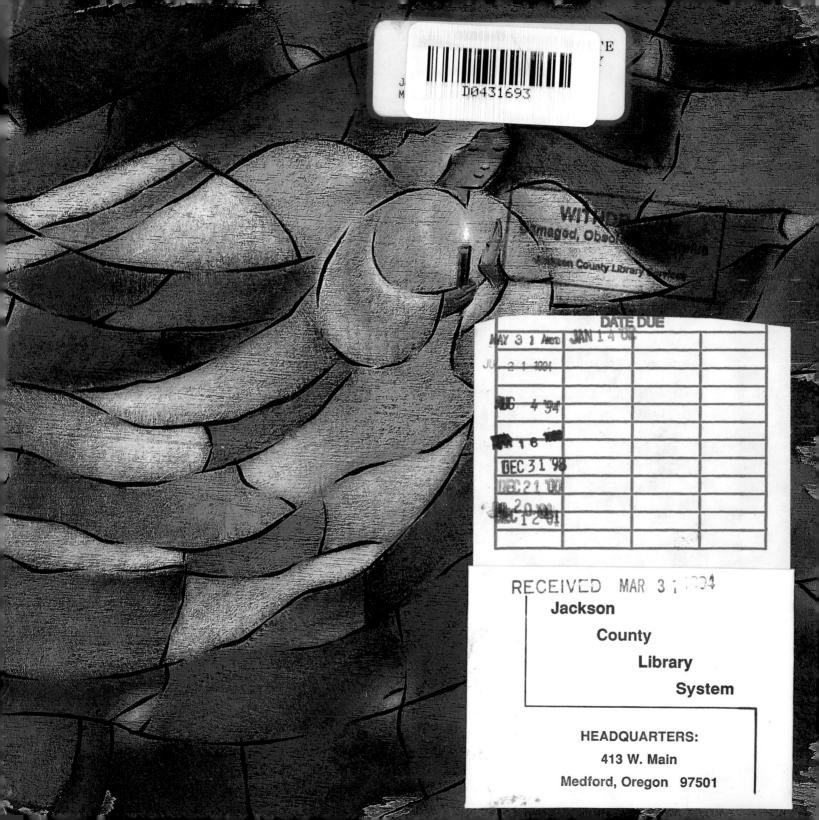

The First Night

by B. G. Hennessy

paintings by Steve Johnson with Lou Fancher

Viking

VIKING
Published by the Penguin Group
Penguin Books USA Inc., 375 Hudson Street, New York, New York 10014, U.S.A.
Penguin Books Ltd, 27 Wrights Lane, London W8 5TZ, England
Penguin Books Australia Ltd, Ringwood, Victoria, Australia
Penguin Books Canada Ltd, 10 Alcorn Avenue, Toronto, Ontario, Canada M4V 3B2
Penguin Books (N.Z.) Ltd, 182–190 Wairau Road, Auckland 10, New Zealand

Penguin Books Ltd, Registered Offices: Harmondsworth, Middlesex, England

First published in 1993 by Viking, a division of Penguin Books USA Inc.

1   3   5   7   9   10   8   6   4   2

Text copyright © B.G. Hennessy, 1993
Illustrations copyright © Steve Johnson and Lou Fancher, 1993
Library of Congress Cataloging-in-Publication Data
Hennessy, B. G. (Barbara G.)
The first night / by B.G. Hennessy; illustrated by Steve Johnson and Lou Fancher.   p.   cm.
Summary: A simple retelling of the birth of Jesus with emphasis on
the quiet time before the arrival of the shepherds, angels, and kings.
I S B N   0 - 6 7 0 - 8 3 0 2 6 - 7
1. Jesus Christ—Juvenile fiction.   [1. Jesus Christ—Nativity—Fiction.]
I. Johnson, Steve, 1960–   ill.   II. Title.
PZ7.H3914Fi   1993   [E]—dc20   93-9659   CIP   AC

Printed in Hong Kong   Set in Caslon Antique

Design by Lou Fancher

About the Art

In preparing the art for the book, butternut wood was chosen for its texture.
The sketch for each painting was drawn on the wood and the lines cut in with a
carving tool, while the outer edge was shaped with a jigsaw. Two layers of gesso
were applied—one white, one black—after which acrylic paints were used.
Sandpaper and a carving tool were used to create a weathered edge. The art was
then photographed and the color transparencies used for reproduction in the book.

And the Word became flesh, and dwelt among us, and we beheld His glory, glory as of the only begotten from the Father, full of grace and truth.

John 1:14

At the edge
of an old and crowded town
there was a field.

In the field
were two shepherds
and their sheep.

As the sheep slept,
a star moved across
the night sky.

The star settled over a stable
in the town below.

In the warm, dark stable
there was a lamb.
There was a cow, too,
and piles of crisp, yellow hay.

Lantern light shone softly
from a rafter above
while a donkey
slept in a corner.

There was a mother, a father, and a baby.
The baby lay on a bed made of hay.

The baby was seeing this world
for the first time.
He saw the swaying lantern,
the donkey, and the woolly lamb.

He felt the night air,
his soft blanket,
his mother's arms,
his father's hands.

And in that warm, dark stable
his life began.

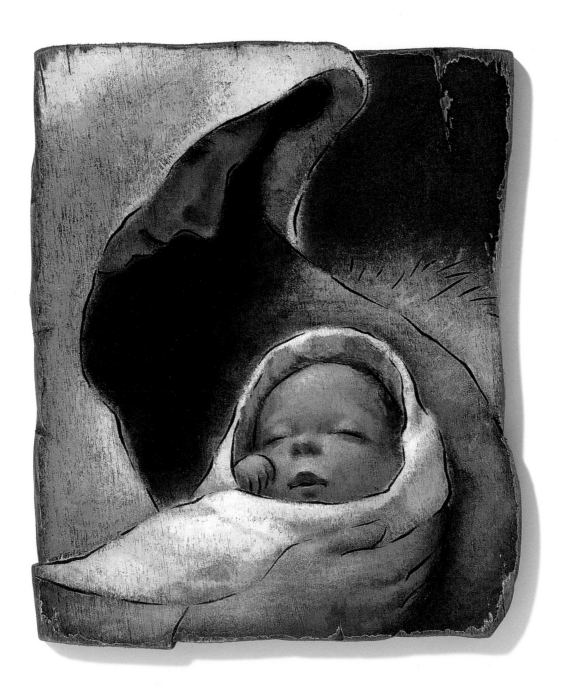

B. G. Hennessy

is the author of eight highly acclaimed books:
The Dinosaur Who Lived in My Backyard; *The Missing Tarts*;
Jake Baked the Cake; *School Days*; *Eeney, Meeney, Miney, Mo*;
A,B,C,D, Tummy, Toes, Hands, Knees;
When You Were Just a Little Girl; and *Sleep Tight*.

Ms. Hennessy grew up on Long Island, New York, and
attended St. Lawrence University and the University of
Wisconsin. She was formerly the art director for a major
New York publisher. She is the mother of three boys, and lives
with her family in Scottsdale, Arizona.

Steve Johnson and Lou Fancher

have collaborated on five children's books. Together they have
illustrated Jon Scieszka's *The Frog Prince, Continued*;
Marsha Wilson Chall's *Up North at the Cabin*; Anne Mazer's
The Salamander Room; and Anna Smucker's *No Star Nights*;
as well as *The First Night*.

Mr. Johnson grew up in Minnesota and studied illustration
and painting at the School of Associated Arts in St. Paul.
Ms. Fancher was born in Michigan and studied art history while
earning her B.F.A. in Dance at the University of Cincinnati.
They are married and live in Minneapolis, Minnesota.